This Little Princess
story belongs to

. . . .

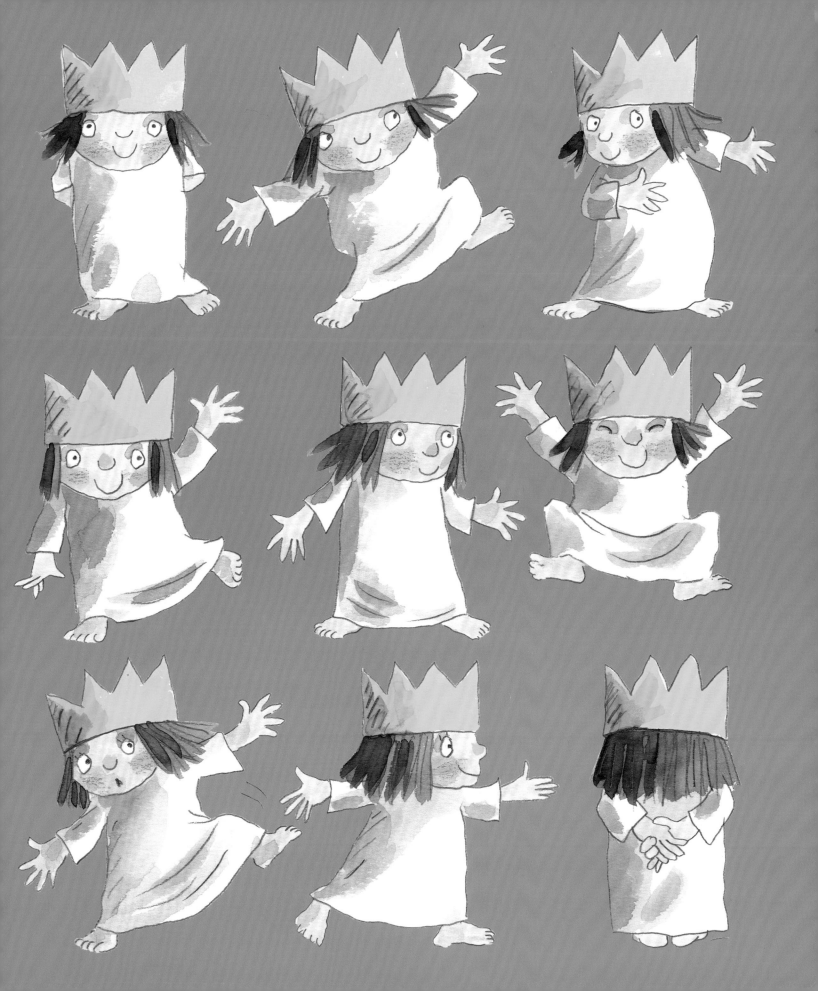

This paperback edition published in 2013 by Andersen Press Ltd.

Published in Australia by Random House Australia Pty., Level 3, 100 Pacific Highway, North Sydney, NSW 2060.

First published in Great Britain in 2002 by Andersen Press Ltd.

Text and Illustration copyright © Tony Ross, 2002

Colour separated in Switzerland by Photolitho AG, Zürich.

Printed and bound in China by Foshan Zhao Rong Printing Co., Ltd.

Tony Ross has used pen, ink and watercolour in this book.

10   9   8   7   6   5   4   3   2   1

British Library Cataloguing in Publication Data available.

ISBN 978 1 84939 536 6 (Trade Edition)

ISBN 978 1 78344 019 1 (Riverside Edition)

A Little Princess Story

I Want My Tooth!

Tony Ross

Andersen Press

The Little Princess had WONDERFUL teeth.

She counted them every morning.
Then she cleaned them . . .

. . . then she counted them again.
She had TWENTY.

Some of her friends had fewer than twenty teeth.
But THEY were not ROYAL.

Her little brother, who WAS royal,
had NO teeth at all.

"Haven't I got wonderful teeth?" said the Little Princess.
"In smart straight lines," said the General.
"Shipshape and Bristol fashion," said the Admiral.

"Haven't I got wonderful teeth?" said the Little Princess.
"ROYAL teeth!" said the King.

So every night, the Little Princess cleaned
the royal teeth again.

"Your wonderful teeth are because
you eat all the right things," said the Cook.

"You can count them if you like," said the Little Princess.
"One . . . two . . . three . . . four . . .

"HEY," said the Cook. "This one WOBBLES!"

"AAAAAGH!" screamed the Little Princess.
"One WOBBLES!"

"AAAAAGH!" screamed the Maid.
"One WOBBLES!"

The wobbly tooth wobbled MORE each day.

But the wobbly tooth didn't hurt, and soon
the Little Princess enjoyed wobbling it.

And she wobbled it and wobbled it, until the terrible
day the wobbly tooth disappeared.

"I WANT MY TOOTH!"
cried the Little Princess.

"You can have mine," said the Dentist,
"until your new one comes along!"
"I want my tooth NOW!" said the Little Princess.

Everybody in the Palace searched for the missing tooth . . .

. . . but it was NOWHERE to be found.
"I WANT MY TOOTH!" cried the Little Princess.

"SHE WANTS HER TOOTH!" cried the Maid.

"It's all right," said the Little Princess.
"I've FOUND it . . .

. . . HE'S got it!"

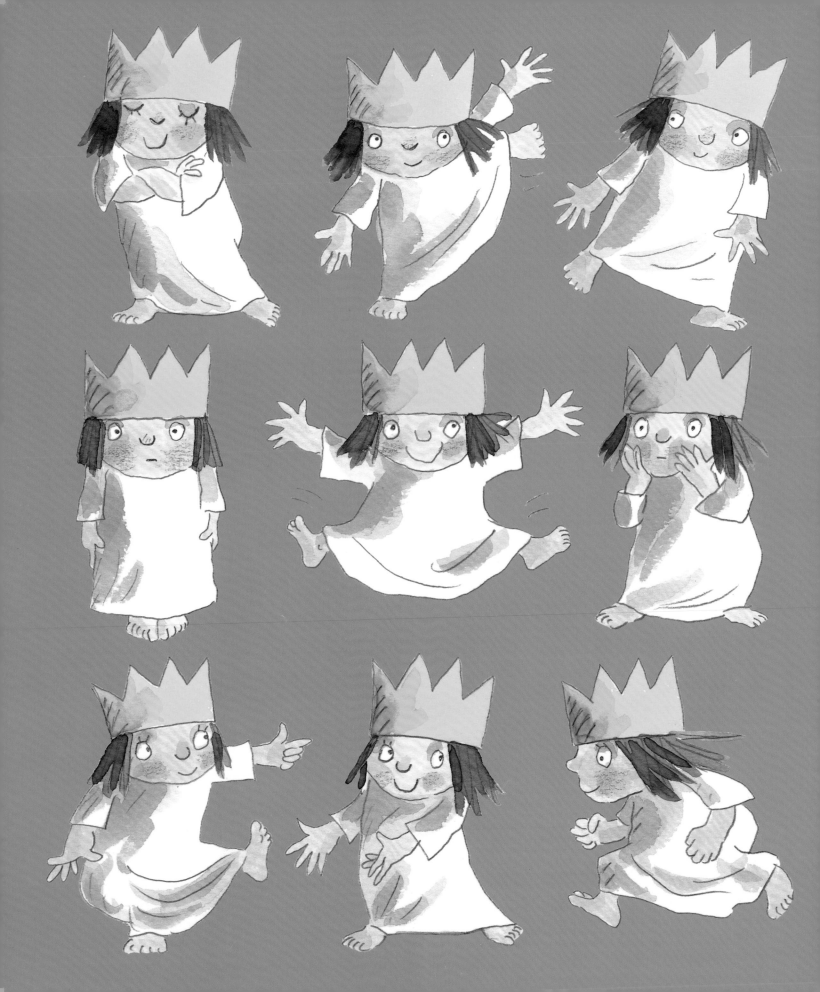

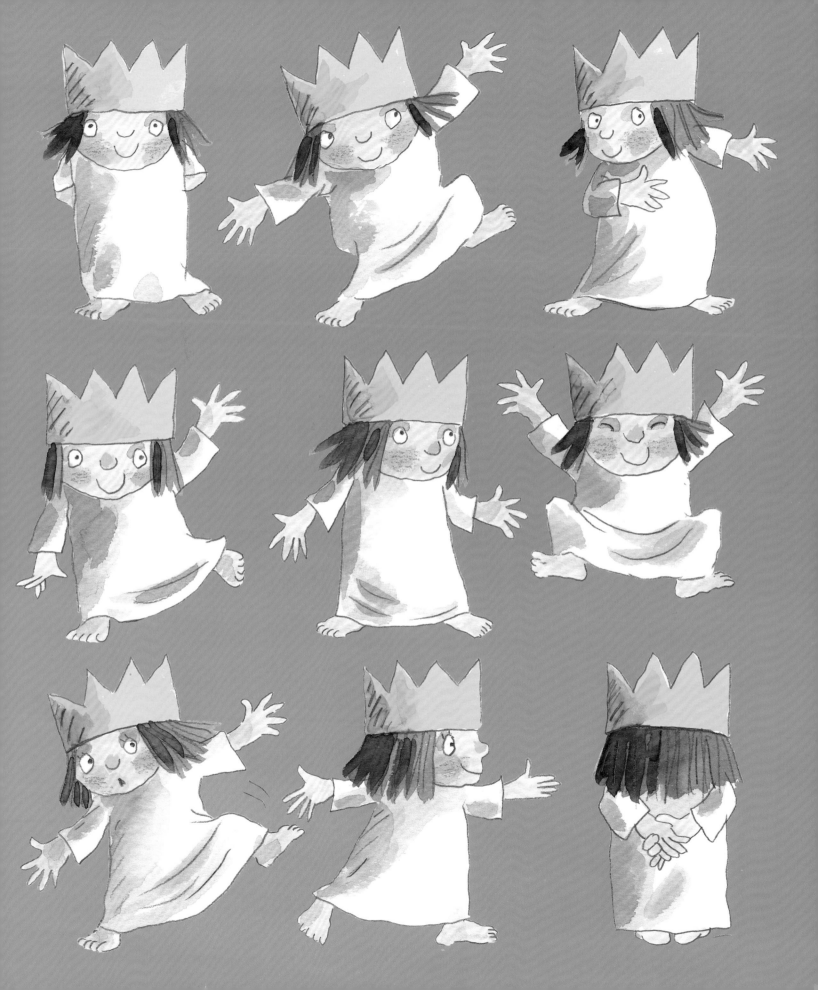

Other Little Princess Books

I Didn't Do it!

I Don't Want to Go to Hospital!

I Don't Want to Wash My Hands!

I Want a Boyfriend!

I Want a Party!

I Want a Sister!

I Want My Dummy!

I Want My Light On!

I Want My Potty!

I Want to Be!

I Want to Do it By Myself!

I Want to Go Home!

I Want to Win!

I Want Two Birthdays!

Little Princess titles are also available as eBooks.

LITTLE PRINCESS TV TIE-INS

Fun in the Sun!

I Want to Do Magic!

I Want My Sledge!

I Don't Like Salad!

I Don't Want to Comb My Hair!

I Want to Go to the Fair!

I Want to Be a Cavegirl!

I Want to Be Tall!

I Want My Sledge! Book and DVD